In the same series
The Big Book of Words for Curious Kids
Curious Kids Go to Preschool

Published in North America by
PEACHTREE PUBLISHERS, LTD.
494 Armour Circle, NE
Atlanta, Georgia 30324

Copyright © 1996 Casterman sa, Tournai

Design by Dominique Mazy
Translated from the French by Vicky Holifield

First North American printing February 1997

10 9 8 7 6 5 4 3 2 1

Manufactured in Belgium

Library of Congress Cataloging-in-Publication Data
Antoine, Héloïse,
        [Grand catalogue des petits vacanciers. English]
        Curious kids go on vacation / created by Héloïse Antoine;
    illustrated by Ingrid Godon. —1st U.S. ed.
                p.   cm. —(Big book of words series; 3rd bk.)
        Summary: Presents vocabulary and accompanying illustrations which identify objects
    and activities related to vacation.
        ISBN 1-56145-143-6 (hc)
        1. Vocabulary—Juvenile literature. 2. Vacations—Terminology—Juvenile literature.
[1. Vocabulary. 2. Vacations.] I. Godon, Ingrid, ill. II. Title. III. Series: Antoine, Héloïse. Big book
of words series: 3rd bk.
PE1449.A5813   1997
428.1—DC20
                                                            96-42511
                                                            CIP
                                                            AC

Curious Kids
Go on Vacation

Another Big Book of Words

Created by Héloïse Antoine
Illustrated by Ingrid Godon

PEACHTREE

ATLANTA

Table of Contents

Packing

On the road

The country

The train

The beach

The ferry

Camping

The mountains

Rainy day

The airport

pajamas

boots

hat

big backpack

raincoat

water wings

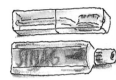
toothbrush
and toothpaste

Packing

duffle bag

suitcase

warm-up suit

sunscreen

toy car

markers

flashlight

backpack

sundress

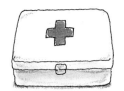
first aid kit

lotto game

hairbrush

shorts

Bobo

plastic sandals

undershirt

socks

sweater

underpants

Legos

tape player

camera

diving mask

cap

ball

beach toys

towels

film

girl's swimsuit

boy's swimsuit

sandals

water bottle

T-shirt

summer skirt

toiletries bag

inner tube

sunglasses

nets

backpack

briefs

beach towel

cookies

road map

tissues

batteries

cooler

nightgown

beach umbrella

mama's purse

coloring book

fanny pack

change purse

shoes

doll

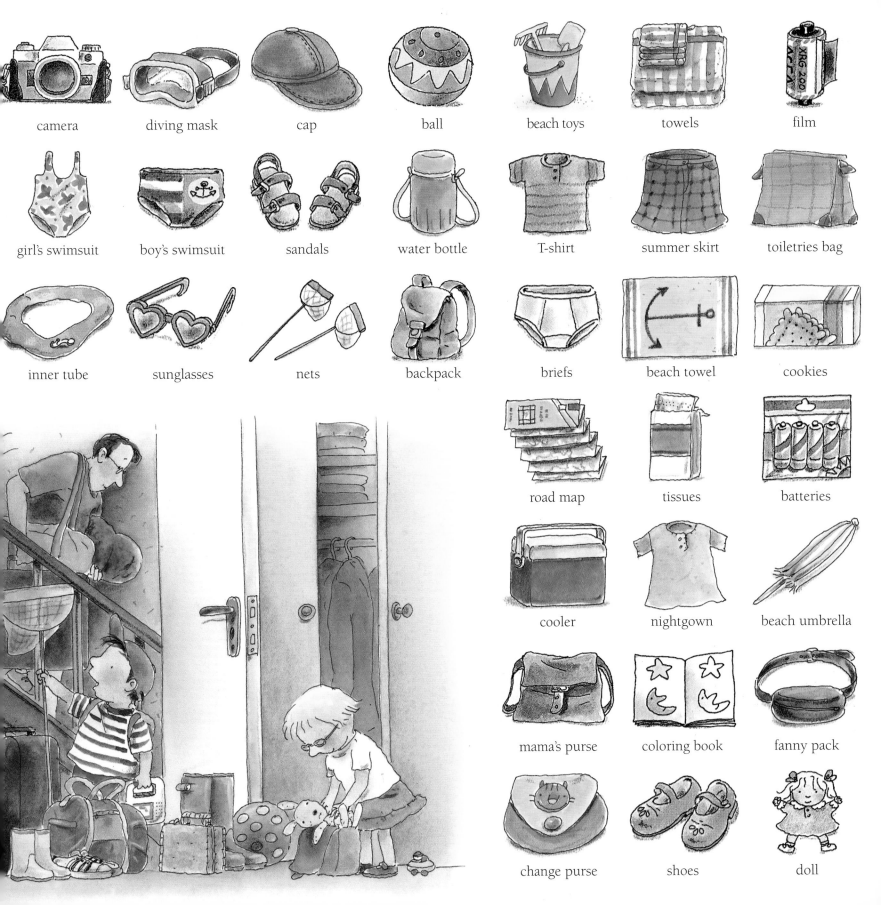

 car and camper

 sunglasses

 car radio

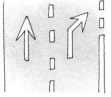 highway

 tow truck

 side view mirror

On the road

 policeman

 sunshade

 travel bed

 cat carrier

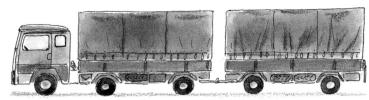 tractor trailer

 "stop"

 carsickness medicine

 RV

 red light

 ambulance

 cookies

 yellow light

 bus

 green light

 motorcycle

 cassette tapes

 steering wheel

rearview mirror

station wagon

horse trailer and four-wheel drive

keys

tollbooth

tape player

police car

gas can

turn signal

headlights

seat belt

Bobo

small car

toy car

boat trailer and minivan

tire

road map

speedometer

gas pump

car seat

car wash

windshield wiper

"animal crossing"

trailer

"rest area"

van

"no entry"

rest area

The country

pheasant

wheat

iris

spider

water lily

buttercup

butterfly

fly

rabbit hutch

rabbit

goat

poppy

bush

dragonfly

balloon

blackbird

duck

sheep

hen and chicks

squirrel

turkey

beehive

robin

horse

fence

hedgehog

earthworm

toy car

butterfly net

picnic blanket

fern

tree

pig

haywagon and tractor

Swiss army knife

thermos

sunflower

picnic utensils

cow

cattails

daisies

heron

four-leaf clover

magpie

frog

snake

bee

fish

lizard

combine harvester

fishing rod

haystack

ant

milk can

nest

picnic basket

weed

Bobo

ladybug

blackberries

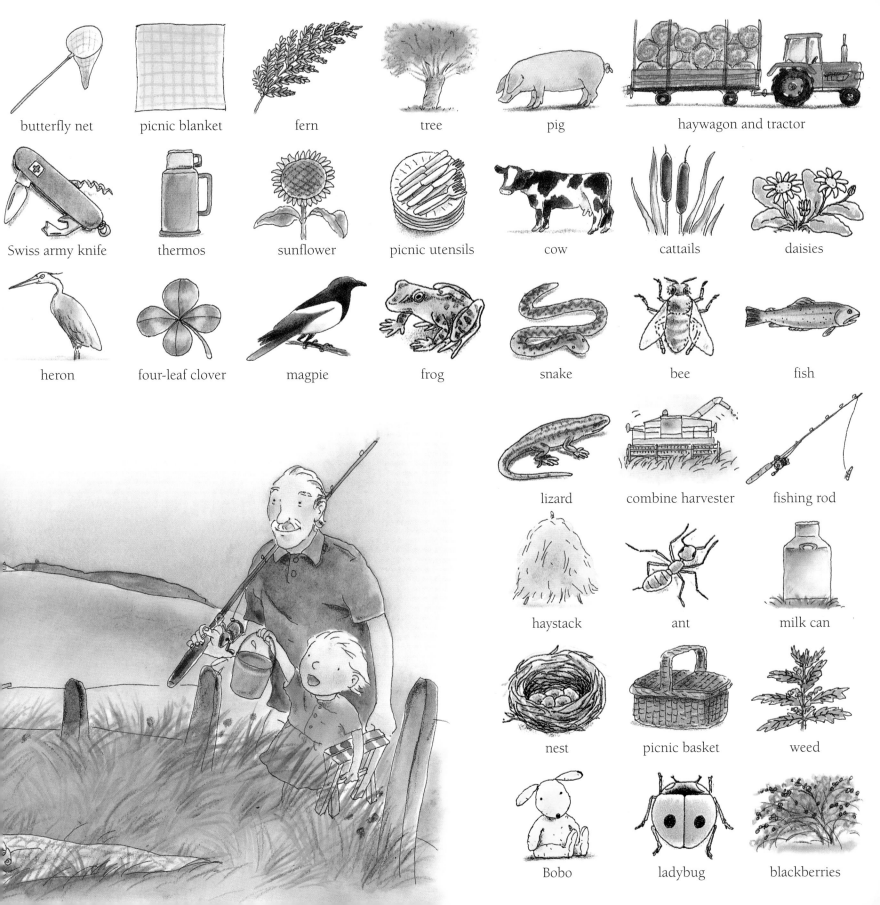

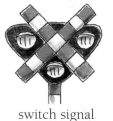 switch signal

 berths

 toy car

 trash can

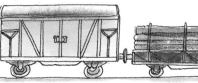 cassette tapes

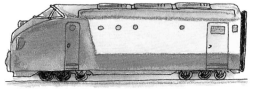 boxcar and flatcar

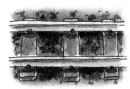 railroad track

The train

 locomotive

 backpack

 coloring book

 cookies

 clock

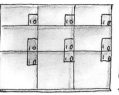 compartment

 lockers

 automobile transport car

 backpack

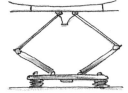 cable connector (pantograph)

 magazines

 railroad switch

 Bobo

 crossing gate

 platform shelter

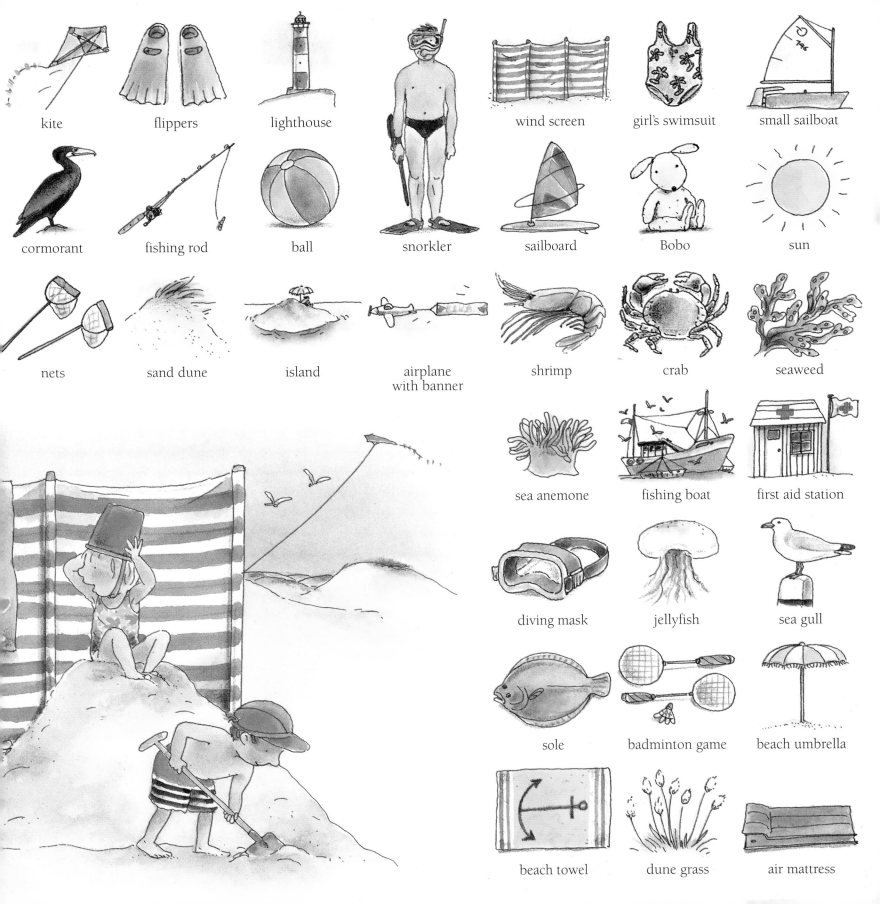

kite

flippers

lighthouse

wind screen

girl's swimsuit

small sailboat

cormorant

fishing rod

ball

snorkler

sailboard

Bobo

sun

nets

sand dune

island

airplane
with banner

shrimp

crab

seaweed

sea anemone

fishing boat

first aid station

diving mask

jellyfish

sea gull

sole

badminton game

beach umbrella

beach towel

dune grass

air mattress

 toy car

 radar

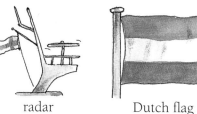 Dutch flag

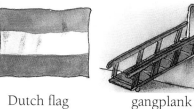 gangplank

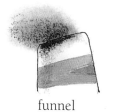 funnel

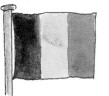 Belgian flag

 backpack

 anchor

The ferry

German flag

 cargo ship

seasick passenger

mooring rope

signal flags

crew member

 sailor

coast

 life jacket

 lifeboat

 dolphin

 British flag

 lighthouse

 mechanic

 ocean liner

Bobo

bridge

foghorn

railing

tugboat

Spanish flag

sea gull

French flag

server

ferry

pier

tape player

buoy

cormorant

United States flag

car

"watch your step!"

berths

"no smoking"

backpack

hovercraft

pirate flag

customs officer

propeller

helm

life preserver

Canadian flag

captain

 sinks

 toilet paper

 sponge

 water bottle

 sleeping bag

 backpack

 folding table

 Swiss army knife

Camping

 camping lantern

 RV

 beach umbrella

 moth

 picnic utensils

 towels and washcloths

 ant

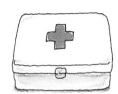 first aid kit

 flashlight

 insect bite ointment

 crescent moon

 pillow

 brush

 air pump

 books

 cup

 mosquito

 plastic containers

 daddy's bicycle

 trash can

soap case

Bobo

family tent

camp stool

cooking pot

frying pan

pop-up tent

mama's bicycle

stars

binoculars

ground mat

flyswatter

camper

tent stakes

nightgown

pajamas

pup tent

toy car

mallet

"camping"

wash basin

big backpack

clothesline

backpack

full moon

camera

air mattress

showers

cooler

barbeque grill

camp stove

campsite number

tape player

 feeding trough

 Bobo

 lake

 rafting

 winding road

 hat

 tunnel

The mountains

 backpack

 falcon

 socks

 helmet

 lookout tower

 fox

 "dangerous descent"

 cable car

 cabin

 bighorn sheep

 bush

wild boar

 toy car

 water bottle

sunscreen

 sheep

 baby carrier

 "falling rocks"

 camera

 road map

 sweater

cap

mountain wildflowers

wild goat

ice axe

hang glider

hiking stick

hiking boots

cow

backpack

rope

Swiss army knife

binoculars

windbreaker

cowbell

viaduct

spring

fences

fir tree

snowcapped peaks

snake

marmot

mountain bike

antelope

fortress

parasail

glacier

valley

horse

chair lift

eagle

pinecone

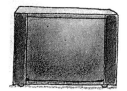
television

VCR

slug

hot chocolate

colored pencils

boots

paintbrush and
water jar

Rainy day

toy car

rain clouds

BIG BOOK OF WORDS

rolling pin

cookie cutters

mushrooms

frog

doll

snail

mud puddles

radio

bag of Legos

jeans

markers

rain hat

stickers

baker's clay

apron

lotto game

tape player

newspaper

Bobo

at the movies

cake

rainspout

cassette tapes

books

rainbow

paint set

raincoat

coloring book

fountain pen

postcards

mud

puzzle

mama's windbreaker

umbrella

daddy's windbreaker

toy car

paper doll chain

sweater

scissors

drawing

staying dry inside

staying dry outside

teapot

cake pan

mama's book

card game

paper towels

socks

carry-on bag

baggage
compartment

baggage claim
ticket

takeoff

control tower

wing

The airport

window

seat belt

radar

customs officer

passport

taxi

metal detector

bus

helicopter

passenger stairs

walkie-talkie

sleeping mask

flight attendant

parachute

oxygen mask

landing gear

flight attendant

airplane hangar

wind sock

arrivals and departures

snack bar

baggage carousel

meal tray

life jacket

baggage cart

baggage security check

airplane

scale

present

vending machine

suitcase

baggage trailers

carry-on bag

fuel truck

airsickness bag

fire truck

newspaper

tray table

headset

tail of the airplane

airplane door

book

emergency slide

ramp worker

serving cart

cockpit

pilot